for Will

First edition for the United States, its territories and dependencies and Canada published in 2005 by Barron's Educational Series, Inc.

First published in Great Britain in 2004 by
Andersen Press, Ltd., 20 Vauxhall Bridge Road
London, SW1V 2SA.

All inquiries should be addressed to:
Barron's Educational Series, Inc.
250 Wireless Blvd.
Hauppauge, NY 11788
www.barronseduc.com

International Standard Book No.: 0-7641-3190-7

Library of Congress Catalog No.: 2004096275

Printed and bound in Italy
9 8 7 6 5 4 3 2 1

Goosie's Good Idea

Peta Coplans

A goose had grown her turnips all winter.

Now she was ready to take them to market.

"I'll sell these turnips," said the goose, "and with the money I make, I can buy a pot to cook in."

Early the next day, she set off.

But the sack of turnips
was very heavy,

and the goose had to sit down and rest.
Along came a cow, carrying
a small piece of cheese.

Market

"Poor Goosie," said the cow,
"I can see those turnips are very heavy.
 Why don't you trade them for
 this delicious piece of cheese?"

"What a good idea!"
said the goose . . .

"Why didn't I think of that?"

Goosie took the cheese and off she went to market.

Very soon, she met a mouse . . .

"Poor Goosie," said the mouse.
"Your cheese is melting in this hot sun.
 I have a fresh sardine here, straight from the sea.
 Let's swap!"

"Good idea! Why didn't I think of that?" said the goose.
She took the sardine and off she went to market.

A passing cat spied the sardine.

"Poor Goosie," he said. "Your sardine is starting to smell.
No one will want to buy it . . .

Have this cup of water, with no smell at all,
and I'll take your stinky old sardine."
"That IS a good idea!" said the goose.
"Why didn't I think of that?"

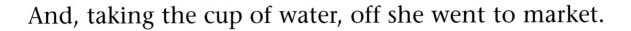

And, taking the cup of water, off she went to market.

She was almost there, when she met a thirsty goat.

"Poor Goosie," said the goat. "You're spilling your water! Besides, the market is right by the river.

I will give you this beautiful stone, and you can leave your cup of water here."

"Now THAT'S a good idea! Why didn't I think of that?" said the goose. She took the stone and off she went.

At last the goose reached the market.
She showed the stone to everyone,
but nobody wanted to buy it.

Fresh
Eggs

She sat down in the shade,
next to a sad-looking duck.

"I wish I could eat these nuts I bought," said the duck,
"but I don't have a stone to crack them."

The goose stopped to think.
"I have a stone," she said happily.
"But what will you give me in return?"

"I have a few turnip seeds," said the duck.
"You could grow a nice crop of turnips to sell next spring."

"Now that's what I call a really GOOD idea!" said the goose . . .

"Then I can buy a pot to cook in!"